This Walker book belongs to:

First published 1976 by Hamish Hamilton Ltd

This edition published 2010 by Walker Books Ltd
87 Vauxhall Walk, London SE11 5HJ

6 8 10 9 7

This book has been typeset in Gill Sans

Printed in China

British Library Cataloguing in Publication Data:
a catalogue record for this book is available from the British Library

ISBN 978-1-4063-2628-4

www.walker.co.uk

THROUGH THE MAGIC MIRROR

Anthony Browne

WALKER BOOKS
AND SUBSIDIARIES
LONDON • BOSTON • SYDNEY • AUCKLAND

Toby sat in the big chair. He was fed up.
Fed up with books, fed up with toys,
fed up with everything.

He went into the living-room.
Nothing was happening there.

Going back upstairs he saw himself in a mirror. Something looked very strange. What was wrong?

He put out his hand to touch the mirror – and walked right through it!

He was out in the street.

It seemed like the same old street, but was it?

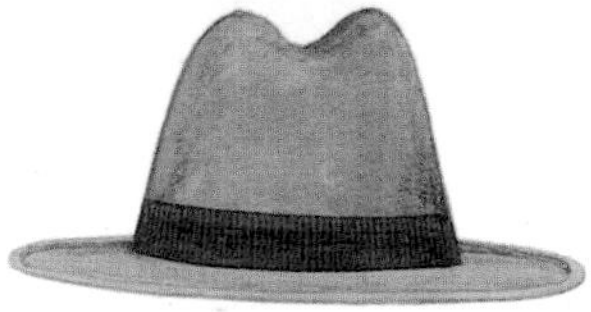

An invisible man passed by.

On the corner was an easel.
On the easel was a painting

of a painting

of a painting.

Just then a dog came along,
taking a man for a walk.

Toby walked on.
Two men were painting a fence.

Toby took another look.
He could hardly believe what he saw.

Suddenly the sky became dark as a flock of choirboys flew overhead.

A terrified cat darted past,
chased by a gang of hungry mice.

And the traffic seemed somehow different.

Across the road Toby saw a poster for the zoo.

But what was happening?

Toby ran as fast as he could.
Where was that mirror?

Of course, there it was,
right behind him.

Toby stepped through, back into his own house.

He turned around and looked at himself in the mirror. When he saw his face, he smiled.

Then he ran
down to tea.

Anthony Browne

Anthony Browne is one of the most celebrated author–illustrators of his generation. Acclaimed Children's Laureate from 2009 to 2011 and winner of multiple awards – including the prestigious Kate Greenaway Medal and the much coveted Hans Christian Andersen Award – Anthony is renowned for his unique style. His work is loved around the world.

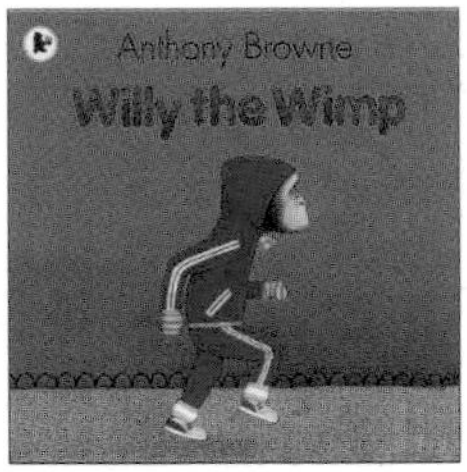

ISBN 978-1-4063-1874-6

ISBN 978-1-4063-1356-7

ISBN 978-1-4063-1357-4

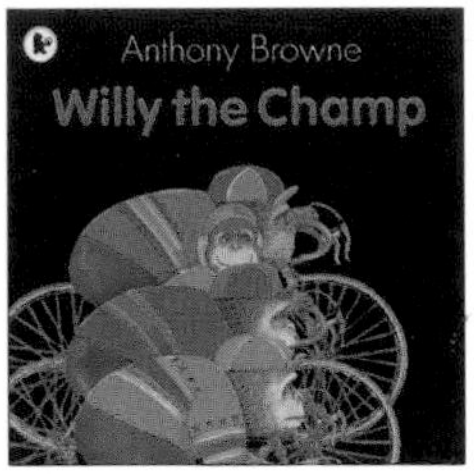

ISBN 978-1-4063-1873-9

ISBN 978-1-4063-1328-4

ISBN 978-1-4063-3851-5
ISBN 978-1-4063-4791-3
Board book edition

ISBN 978-0-7445-9858-2
ISBN 978-1-4063-2187-6
Board book edition

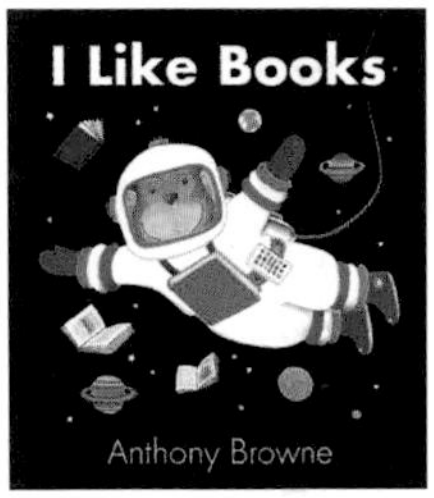

ISBN 978-0-7445-9857-5
ISBN 978-1-4063-2178-4
Board book edition

ISBN 978-1-4063-0576-0

ISBN 978-1-84428-559-4

ISBN 978-1-4063-5233-7

ISBN 978-1-4063-1930-9

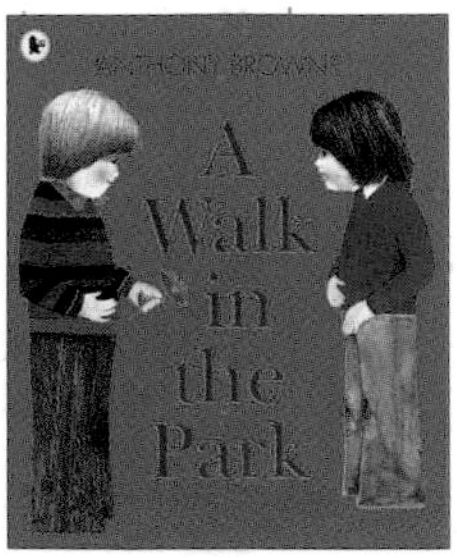

ISBN 978-1-4063-4164-5

ISBN 978-1-4063-4162-1

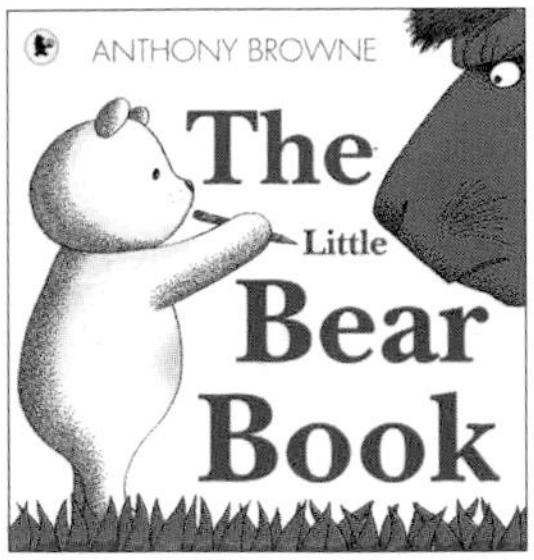

ISBN 978-1-4063-4163-8

Available from all good booksellers

www.walker.co.uk